DOG PARADE

Barbara Joosse

Pictures by Eugene Yelchin

Harcourt Children's Books
Houghton Mifflin Harcourt
Boston   New York   2011

Harcourt Children's Books is an imprint of
Houghton Mifflin Harcourt Publishing Company.

www.hmhbooks.com

The illustrations in this book were done in gouache on watercolor paper.
The text type was set in Bryant Regular.
The display type was set in Zebrawood.
Design by Christine Kettner and Opal Roengchai

Library of Congress Cataloging-in-Publication Data
Joosse, Barbara M.
Dog parade / written by Barbara Joosse; pictures by Eugene Yelchin.
p. cm.
Summary: Dogs of all sizes, shapes, and personalities come together with their humans to don
costumes and participate in a parade.
ISBN 978-0-15-206690-1
[1. Dogs—Fiction. 2. Parades—Fiction.] I. Yelchin, Eugene, ill. II. Title.
PZ7.J7435Dog 2012
[E]—dc22
2010043399

Manufactured in Singapore
TWP 10 9 8 7 6 5 4 3 2 1
4500288184

For Mina Mina Trampolina,
who is full full FULL of
sparkling adventure —B.J.

For Bird —E.Y.

Everybody's coming—

furry ones

barky ones

running-in-the-parky ones.

So don't drag your tail!

Get on your getup

and put your best paw forward.

Excuse me, **barkbarkbark!**
I'm Tinkles. Gotta pee.

What's in the bag? Gotta pee again.

grrrrrrrr!

barkbarkbark!

Is that my costume? Lemme see. Gotta . . .

WHEEE!

Howdy-do.

I'm Gracie-Pants.

Don'tcha love my smoky eyes—bat bat?

Don'tcha love my dainty ears—flap flap?

Lah-Dee-Dah.

Is this for little old me?

Darlin'!

It's . . .

CHARMIN'!

Slurp.
I was in the pound, and you found me.
You named me **LOVIE**.

For you,
I can bring the newspaper
without chewing it (usually).

I can bring your sneakers and only take a tiny taste.

I can tell the squirrel, **WATCH OUT! WATCH OUT!**

and guard the baby

and bring in the mail

and tell you the pot is boiling

because I'm your very own . . .

WONDER

DOG!

FRITZIE in charge.

All right, people.

Over here. Over there.

Ready . . . hup! Line up!

ONE-TWO-THREE-FOUR, ONE-TWO-**THREE-FOUR!**

Hrumph.

You want me to wear . . . this?

Wouldn't a uniform be more appropriate?

Medals. RIBBONS. STARS.

So on and so forth.

But . . . ach. You are my Dumpling
and I've made you smile.
As you wish. I will be your . . .

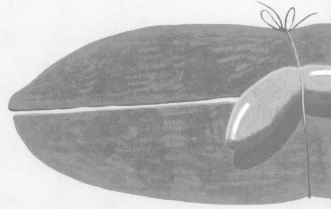

WEENIE!

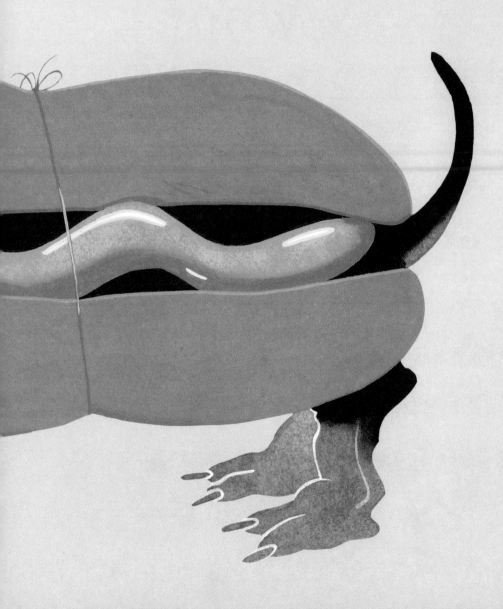

Woof.

It's me, **WALTER.**

I should be fierce. I know that.
But could I hide behind your leg?

Oh, no! A costume?

And a parade?

But I don't want anyone to see me.

I want to disappear!

Is this it?

Thank you.

I'm a . . .

GHOST.

Here I come! I'm Comet!

Ooooooh. There's something in the dirt.

diggitydig diggity

Ooooooh. You had something good for lunch.

licketylick lickety

So much to do do doooooo.

Wriggle into this. Put that on my head.

I'm . . .

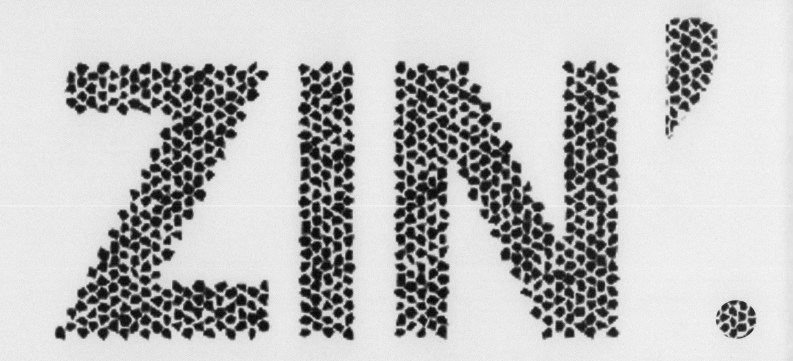

ZIN'.

A-a-aaaaaooooo!

I'm Ike.

What?

I have to wear this?

No-no-naaaaooooo!

I do not like those things.

They have names like Muffin and Cuddles

and prance around like Little Miss Smartypants.

People think they're cute.

Peeeuw.

MEEEUW!

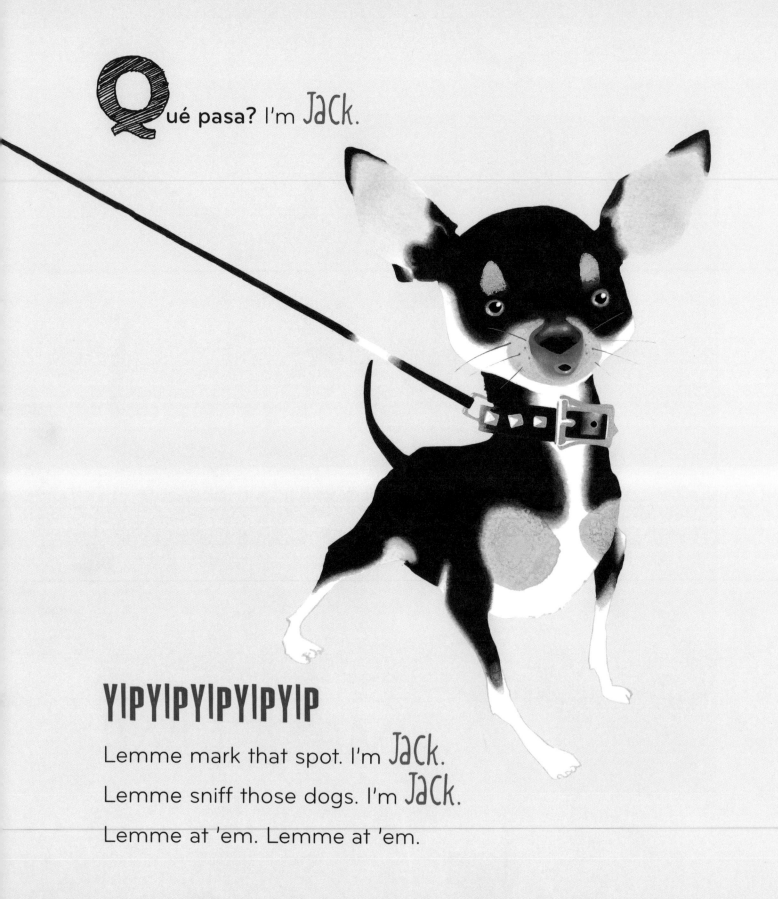

Qué pasa? I'm Jack.

YIPYIPYIPYIPYIP

Lemme mark that spot. I'm Jack.

Lemme sniff those dogs. I'm Jack.

Lemme at 'em. Lemme at 'em.

I'm Jack. **YIP!**

You want me to come?

No dice.

You want me to be quiet?

No can do.

You want me to . . .

Uh-oh . . .

BUSTED!

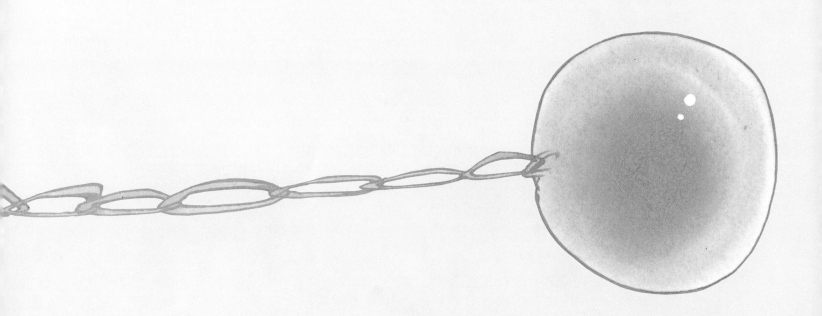

WE'RE ON PARADE!

We came to show off
our diggity best.

We're wonder dogs, weenies, and ghosts—
for YOU! Our humans.
THE ONES WE LOVE MOST!

Furever and ever!